CHARLIE'S TANGLE

Dyslexic Friendly Edition

Tif E. Boots

Illustrated by Syranity Barker

Copyright © 2023 by Tif E. Boots
Illustrations © 2023 Syranity Barker
Cover Design © 2023 by Evelyn Rainey
Dyslexic Friendly Typography © 2025 by Rolland Kenneson

ISBN-13: 978-1-963272-24-6

ShelteringTree.Earth, LLC Publishing
PO Box 973, Eagle Lake, FL 33839

Visit our website: ShelteringTreeMedia.com

Did you enjoy this book?

We love to hear from our readers.

Please visit the author at https://bootsbooks.net/

What is a "Dyslexic Friendly" Book?

Sheltering Tree Media has taken steps to make our books more friendly for those who live with dyslexia. While the following principles will not make every book readable for every reader, it is our best effort to create products that encourage reading and to support all readers.

Throughout the book, we use a font named OpenDyslexic. This is a free font that is designed to help dyslexic readers distinguish each letter from the others. For more information about OpenDyslexic, how it differs from other fonts, and research behind the font, visit their website: www.opendyslexic.com.

The space between each word is increased (this is called *word spacing*). This helps better to distinguish when one word ends and the next begins. The line spacing is greater than most common fonts (this is called *leading*). This all should help with readability.

Whenever possible, the text is Left-Aligned but it is not justified on the right side. Allowing the right side of a paragraph to remain *rough* keeps the word spacing consistent throughout.

Our Dyslexic Friendly books are printed on cream or ivory paper which is also thicker than the average book page. This minimizes the sharp contrast of black-on-white pages as well as bleedthrough of text from the previous page.

Finally, Sheltering Tree Media has made colored overlays available when you purchase a book through our online store. You can find these overlays at ShelteringTreeMedia.com/shop/dyslexic-friendly.

These are some of the principles we use to create a book as readable as possible to those living with dyslexia. Some may find this helpful; some may not. Please provide us with any insights you might have to improve our Dyslexic Friendly principles. We pray this will enable many to heighten their love for reading.

DEDICATION

For all the children in my life.
Kindness never goes
out of style.

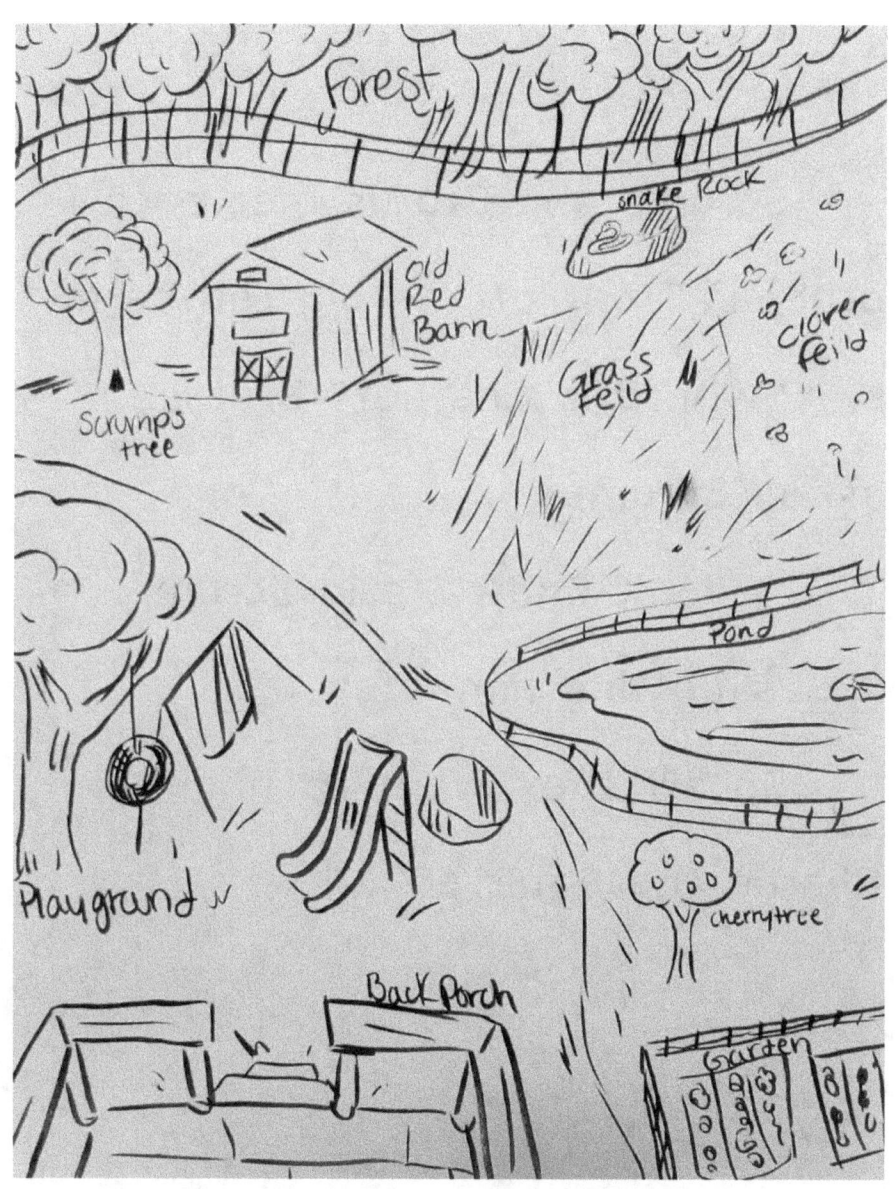

Scrump and Brutus met each other in front of the big red barn.

"Where is Charlie?" Brutus asked Scrump.

"I don't know," said Scrump. "Let's go find him."

So off they went to find Charlie the Squirrel.

They circled around the barn and started to walk toward the pond when they heard, "Help, help me please!"

"That sounds like Charlie," said Brutus.

"Charlie? Where are you?" called Scrump.

"I'm up here, stuck in a tree!" cried Charlie. "My tail is tangled in some ribbon."

Brutus and Scrump looked way up. In the top of a tree, they saw Charlie hanging upside down by his tail.

"Don't worry," cheered Scrump.

"We will get you down," promised Brutus.

Scrump and Brutus thought for a minute.

"How are we going to get him down?" asked Scrump. "We can't climb a tree."

"What happens when he falls after we get his tail unstuck?" Brutus worried. "That's a long way down."

They sat and thought. They walked around the tree and thought. They craned their necks and looked way up and still they thought.

"We could throw rocks at the branch Charlie is stuck on and break the branch," suggested Scrump.

"That might work, but it could hurt Charlie if we hit him," Brutus said.

"We could find someone to tie a rope to the branch and then pull it down," Scrump tried again.

"I think we are going to need to find help any ways, but if we break the branch Charlie can still get hurt in the fall," fretted Brutus.

"Yeah," agreed Scrump, "We need to come up with a safe plan for this rescue."

They sat and thought some more.

"I know," Brutus soon exclaimed, "We can go to the woods and see if we can find someone that can climb to cut him down."

"That's a good start," said Scrump. "We can't do this alone, but that doesn't help with getting him down safely after we get him loose."

They thought some more.

"Maybe we can make a big pile of leaves for him to land in," Scrump's nose twitched with excitement.

"That would work, but even with a lot of help, I think that may take too long," Brutus sighed.

"I guess so," Scrump agreed. "That would be a lot of leaves to find and move. Charlie must be super dizzy already."

"I watched my human hang a blanket outside today. Maybe we can borrow that to catch Charlie in."

"Oh, that's a super good idea!" Scrump began to run. "I'll go to the woods and find help. You can go get the blanket."

Brutus went to the cloths line and jumped up to catch the blanket with his teeth. The wind blew and he missed it. He tried again and again but the blanket kept moving in the wind.

"You get the master's clean linen dirty and they won't be happy," growled a voice from behind him.

Brutus turned around to see Dash the black lab standing behind him.

"Dash, boy am I glad to see you. My friend Charlie is stuck in a tree. I need this so we can catch him when we get him unstuck," Brutus explained.

"Well," said Dash, "That seems like a good reason to borrow the master's clean linen. I'll help you get it down."

Dash jumped up once and caught the blanket with his teeth. Then he tugged until it fell to the ground.

Brutus picked up part of the blanket and they both carried it back to the tree where Charlie was still hanging upside down.

Scrump was running through the woods. "Help! Please help!" he shouted. "My friend is stuck in a tree."

"I will help," he heard the bushes say. Scrump stopped running and stared at the bush. A pair of yellow eyes stared right back at him. Scrump backed away and was ready to run when a fox stepped out of the thicket.

Scrump turned and jumped away, but the fox caught him. "Why are you fleeing?" asked the fox "Didn't you just call for help?"

"Ye..ye..Yes" stuttered Scrump, "But you're a fox and foxes eat rabbits."

"I'm not going to eat you," said the fox. "My name is Lawrence. I was going to help you."

"Oh. Okay," said Scrump and he told Lawrence about his friend Charlie who was tangled in a tree.

"Well," said Lawrence, "I can't climb a tree but I know someone who can fly to the top of it." Lawrence barked loudly. "Twitter!"

From high above, a hawk flew over and landed on a low tree branch. Lawrence told Twitter Scrump's problem and all three of them went back to the tree where Charlie was stuck.

Brutus, Scrump, Lawrence, Dash, and Twitter met together under the tree. Brutus introduced Dash. Scrump introduced Lawrence. Lawrence introduced Twitter. All the while, Charlie dangled from his tail high above them, swinging in the wind.

Charlie shouted, "It is very nice to meet all of you, but would you mind hurrying up!"

They sat or perched and came up with the next step of the plan to get Charlie down.

"Everyone can grab a corner and pull the blanket tight," woofed Dash. "That will work for a safe landing I think."

"Twitter can fly up and cut the ribbon," yapped Lawrence. "And we can catch Charlie when he falls."

"Those are fantastic ideas!" Scrump thumped his feet.

Dash, Lawrence, Brutus, and Scrump all grabbed a part of the blanket and pulled.

Twitter flew up to Charlie and cut the ribbon with her sharp beak.

Down fell Charlie who landed with a soft *thwonk* sound into the blanket his friends were holding.

"Thank you all," chittered Charlie. "Together, you make a great team."

After Charlie was safely back on the ground, they all returned the blanket the back porch. Brutus and his friends, new and old, played together.

"Today has been a lot of fun," said Scrump as the sun sank behind the trees.

"It was also a little scary," laughed Charlie.

"We all made a good rescue team," replied Brutus. "But I hope we do not have to rescue anyone again tomorrow."

Together they laughed and told each other goodnight.

ABOUT THE AUTHOR

Tif E. Boots wrote her first children's book as a birthday present for her daughter. Many years later it has been shared with her sister, cousins, classmates and now you.

Tif was raised in Marana, Arizona and was working concession stands at county fairs in Arizona and Michigan with her family until she graduated from Marana High School in 2000. She became a mother and correctional officer in 2004. She then moved to Nevada, Missouri with her family where she was blessed with her second daughter and fell into a career of nurse's assistant for Hospice.

Tif and her family relocated to Mulberry, Florida in 2017. In her free time, Tif can usually be found on the water or at amusement parks spending time with family and friends and simply enjoying the life that God has blessed her with.

ABOUT THE ILLUSTRATOR

Syranity Barker is an illustrator who has always had a love for art. She was born in Tucson, Arizona and eventually moved to central Florida where she graduated high school.

Syranity illustrated her love of drawing early in life; her family were great supporters of her passions and always made sure she had a variety of supplies and mediums. While still in high school, her work was entered in numerous art shows. She received the *City Commissioners Choice Award* for a mixed media portrait of her dog and has sold several pieces of her work.

Still fresh out of high school, Syranity works two jobs and illustrates professionally in her spare time. She is currently the in-house illustrator for *ShelteringTree.Earth Publishing* and also promotes herself as a free-lance artist.

Syranity enjoys singing, skating, spending time with her friends and family, and creating her own characters and writing backstories for them.

Syranity aspires to become an art teacher and share her passion for drawing and self-expression with others.

DISCUSSION GUIDE FOR CLASSROOMS, SMALL GROUPS, AND INDIVIDUAL STUDY

1. Why do Brutus and Scrump go looking for Charlie?

2. What do they hear on their walk to the pond?

3. Where do they find Charlie?

4. How did Charlie get stuck in a tree?

5. What ideas did they have to get Charlie down?

6. What were the reasons not to use those ideas?

7. Why does Brutus go to get a blanket?

8. Why does Scrump go into the woods by himself?

9. Who helps Brutus at the clothesline?

10. Who does Scrump meet in the woods?

11. Why is Scrump afraid of who he meets?

12. Who do they get the ribbon cut to free Charlie?

13. What do they use to catch Charlie when he falls?

_____

_____

_____

_____

_____

_____

_____

_____

_____

14. What do the friends do after Charlie is rescued?

15. Can you think of another way they could have rescued Charlie?

_____

_____

_____

_____

_____

_____

_____

_____

SEQUENCE SKILLS

Answer each question by drawing or writing in the blue boxes.

What happened first?

Which picture happened second?

Which picture happened third?

What happened next?

Which picture happened last?

What happened after
this picture?

What happened
before this picture?

Put these pictures in order.

Why did Twitter appear in the story before Charlie got free?

What would have happened if Charlie had dropped before Brutus thought about the blanket?

How did Charlie get tangled?

First,

Second,

Then, _____

What else could
Lawrence have done?

What else could
Twitter have done?

What will their next
adventure be?

Tell the story in your own words. Make sure to keep things in order!

SHELTERING TREE

Earth
Publishing
ShelteringTreeMedia.com